S0-CJP-007

SWEET PEA'S TALE OF TOO MANY TOMATOES!

MARCIA LEITER

Sweet Pea Tales
Book 1

Sweet Pea's Tale of TOO MANY TOMATOES!

Story, Illustrations, and Book Design by Marcia Leiter

ISBN 978-0-9970626-1-8

Other books by Marcia Leiter:
Sweet Pea's Christmas
Sweet Pea's Voyage

Visit Sweet Pea at
sweet-pea.net

Dedicated to

Who never grew **too** many tomatoes
and

Who made the **best** gazpacho

Once there was a little bunny who lived in a tidy hole by the stream on the south side of the meadow.

Her name was Sweet Pea.

It was dinnertime. "I will fix spaghetti," she said. She boiled the water and cooked the noodles, then went to fetch the sauce.

She searched high...

...and low...

...but no spaghetti sauce.
She had to eat cold, dry sticky spaghetti.
"This just won't do!" she said.

Then she had an **idea**.

"I will plant tomatoes and **make** spaghetti sauce!" she said.

So the next morning she hopped into her boat
and floated downstream to Town.

This is what she bought.

With much confidence, Sweet Pea prepared her garden, hoed a row and carefully patted the tiny seeds into the soil.

Then she watered them well....

...and went to bed. She dreamed of a mountain of spaghetti covered with rich red tomato sauce.

The days passed. The sun warmed her garden and gentle rains fell. Sweet Pea checked every few hours, but nothing happened. She said...

"Those were bad seeds! Tomorrow I will get my money back!"

But the next day on the way to the "potting shed"
she saw a haze of green. Little seedlings had sprouted!

Each day, Sweet Pea watered and weeded the baby plants.
She devised numerous methods of staking them.
But they did not flower.

So she fertilized them and mulched them and watered them some more.

They grew and **grew** and **grew** until they were TALLER than Sweet Pea!

But her giant plants made no tomatoes.

Sweet Pea **tossed** her tools behind the shed
and **stomped** into the house.

The days passed. Spring turned into summer and Sweet Pea got busy.

She swept her house.

She made new clothes.

She went shopping.

She went to the beach.

She wrote lots and lots of letters. And every Tuesday

she went to visit String Bean
who lived way on the other side of the meadow.

Sweet Pea forgot all about tomatoes.

Then, one day, as she was washing up the dishes, she looked out her window and saw something RED!

Sweet Pea sat down right there in the garden
and ate it like an apple. It was delicious.

The next day there were **2** tomatoes.
She made a sandwich.

The day after that there were **4** and she made tomato pie.

Then with **8** she made tomato soup

and with **16** she made tomato juice.

Soon there were enough tomatoes to make eight dozen bottles of ketchup...

...and 128 jars of spaghetti sauce!

But the tomatoes kept coming! Finally Sweet Pea said

She was about to get grumpy again
but instead she called String Bean.

Together they hatched a plan.

For a
whole week
they
made posters,
wrote letters,
and called friends.
They sawed
and hammered
and cut
and stitched...

...and picked tomatoes!

Sweet Pea was soooo tired of tomatoes, but finally they were ready for the big day.

TWEEET!
TOMATO FEST
ON
MONDAY
AT
TWO
O'CLOCK!!

EC
J
J
B
E
CAKES
ELIZABETH'S BAKERY
JULIE'S JAMS
QUENTIN + the BETTER BOY BAND
ELLE'S HERB
PB + TOMA
JELLY SAND
OMATO COOKIES
TOMATO CAK
TO PIES
POP
TAP TAP
WELCOME
TOMATO FEST
DON'T GO HOME WITHOUT SOME!!!!
FOOD
RIDES
GAMES
PRIZES
BOOTHS
ZZZZZ
ZZZZ

There were booths...

...and games...

TOMATO TOSS
SCORE
TIERRA
DEANDRE
RITA
DARNELL
MARIA
EBONY
TOMATO BOWL
TOMATO RELAY
CHERRY TOMATO HUNT
1ST PRIZE - BUSHEL
2ND - 1/2 BUSHEL
3RD - PECK
4TH - 1/2 PECK
OXX'S BOXES

...and rides...
TOMMY'S TERRIBLE TOMATO-COASTER
TOMATO BALLOON RIDES
ISABELLA'S DIZZY TOMAT
RIDE TICKETS 5¢
NANCY'S 1ST AID
YOU MUST be THIS TALL
HAYRIDE to TOMATO PATCH 5¢ FREE!
PICK-UR-OWN BUSHELS ONLY

CHEEEP!
ALL YOU CAN EAT
SPAGHETTI
5¢
EEK
UH OH
PAT PAT
SLUUURP
SHLUP

...and food!

By evening there was not
a single tomato left.

Sweet Pea and String Bean were beat.

The next day after dinner String Bean said,
"That was fun! Let's do it again next year!"

Sweet Pea said, "No more tomatoes! I will **not** grow **any** more tomatoes **ever** again as long as I live!"

And she didn't.

BIG EAR
BISTRO
FREE
ZUCCHINIS!
ZZZZZZZ
THE
END

About the Author-Illustrator

Marcia Leiter lives in a house by a road in the middle of a garden, with a yard that becomes a meadow when not mowed. Sometimes mice scamper about in the attic. She has been known to grow too many tomatoes. And hot peppers. And eggplants. Her family and friends take them with a smile. This book is for them, and friends of Sweet Pea everywhere. There are more Sweet Pea stories to come...

Sweet Pea's TOMATO Recipes

Welcome to my kitchen! Here are some of the tasty dishes I made in the story. They are easy. I do not measure anything... that gives you lots of leeway. Have fun!

TOMATO SANDWICH

One Grown-up
Whole grain roll, split
Thin cheese slices
Tomato slices
Lettuce

Lightly toast the roll top/bottom
Put cheese on both parts
Broil it till cheese is melted
Layer tomatoes and lettuce
Put the cap on
Eat it (must remove mouse first)

TOMATO SOUP or SPAGHETTI SAUCE

A Grown-up
An onion
Some garlic
Fresh basil
Oregano
Chopped tomatoes

Saute the onion in olive oil
Add the garlic and oregano
Add the tomatoes and basil
Simmer til it looks & smells good
Ladle into a bowl (that is not cracked)
Sprinkle with parmesan, salt, pepper, & croutons

A TOO MANY TOMATOES SEEK & FIND

 A tiny mailbox

A toasty meecemallow 

A worm in an apple

Ants on the honey! 

11 1/2 o'clock ?

A black hat on sale

A pet caterpillar 

A baby in a rebozo

A mistaken identity 

Polka-dot swim trunks

A tiny green knapsack

Grandma knitting 

Green galoshes

A sleeping hatchling 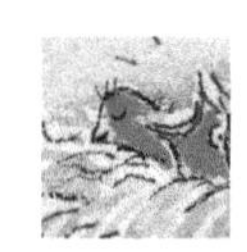

A purple  mouse hoe

A black and white cow 

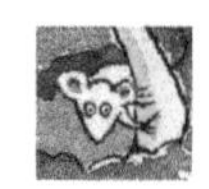 A frightened mouse

A criss-cross  pocket

 Meece blue jeans

An accident with salt 

 A princess in a tower

A tiny bunny happy face

A crawling ladybug 

 A purple butterfly

A pair of flip flops 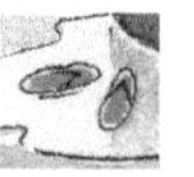

 Bottle of Bunny Bubbles

Nose sniffing 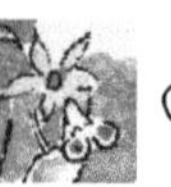 a flower

A Band-Aid blanket 

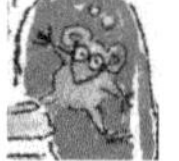 Swimming in the sauce

Little green buttons 

 A green mouse

A mouse scrubbing up 

A teensy  yellow cap

A red and yellow snake

A red lollipop

Contented baby bluebird

An angry white mouse

A very naughty bunny

A friendly orange  fish

A wheelchair wheel

A brown teddy-bunny

An artist  at work

A square red flag

A diaper is changed

A tiny blue  mouse dress

A blue ribbon

A yellow pencil

A bunny in trouble

A stubbed  mouse toe

I don't want to ride!!

A bunny feeling sick

Bunnytot  being fed

A mama saying "NO"

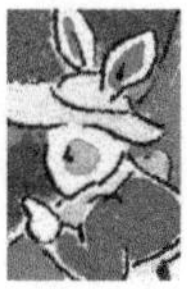

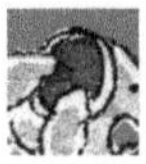

A blue yamaka

A very upset  mama

Two 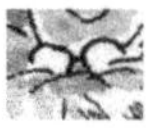 round eggs

A discarded book

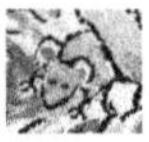

A sleeping gray mouse

A bee not  watching out!

Yellow bow, Red bow

A smiling 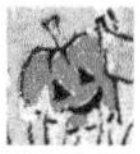 jack-o-lantern

Tulips on a dress

A carrot halfway eaten

Pink mouse eating peas

A  plaid shirt

A wooden sign says

HOW TO GROW TOMATOES

In early spring go to the store.

Buy some
potting soil and
a pack of seeds.

Find a container with holes in the bottom.
Fill it with soil and pat it down.

Poke holes in the
soil and plant
the seeds.
Cover them
with soil
and pat down.

Water the pot

Place it in a warm sunny window and keep it moist.

After the seeds sprout, thin to 1 plant per pot.

In mid spring plant the seedlings out in the garden in a sunny spot. Then do what Sweet Pea did.

Enjoy your tomatoes!

Don't miss these Sweet Pea Tales. Then look for more to come!

Written and illustrated by Marcia Leiter

SWEET PEA'S CHRISTMAS

SWEET PEA TALES Book 2

In this second tale in the series, Sweet Pea's friends and relations decide to visit for the holidays. As the Guest Tally grows, she finds there is more and more to do! Will she be ready by Christmas Day? Will String Bean be able to help out when an unexpected calamity ruins all her plans? Find out, as SWEET PEA'S CHRISTMAS unfolds one day at a time just like an Advent Calendar.

Includes CRAFTS, a Gingerbunny RECIPE and lots of things to SEEK and FIND.

Sweet Pea gets a SURPRISE

Up in the attic

What is the problem?

SWEET PEA'S JOURNEY

SWEET PEA TALES Book 3

In this third tale in the series, Sweet Pea is fed up! Her Christmas Hospitality has left her home a big mess and she wants to get out of there! She tosses a few necessities into her boat and sails South searching for warmer waters. One misadventure after another does not deter Sweet Pea from continuing bravely onward. Will she reach her destination? How many friends will she collect along the way? Sail along with Sweet Pea on this unlikely journey...

Written and illustrated by Marcia Leiter

Included: Make an Origami Boat, I Spy Travel Games, Seek & Find

After the Holidays

She's on her way!

Uh Oh! What happened?

CPSIA information can be obtained
at www.ICGtesting.com
Printed in the USA
LVHW052259161019
634422LV00002B/4/P